In memory of my grandmother, Kate Terry Sellers,
and in honor of my splendid sister, Katharine Broach Bragg
– M.M.

For Anthony and Alison
– I.B.

Text copyright © 2006 by Marni McGee
Illustrations copyright © 2006 by Ian Beck

First published in the United States of America in 2006 by
Walker Publishing Company, Inc.
Distributed to the trade by Holtzbrinck Publishers

First published in Great Britain in 2006 by Bloomsbury Publishing Plc.

For information about permission to reproduce selections from
this book, write to Permissions, Walker & Company,
104 Fifth Avenue, New York, New York 10011.

Library of Congress Cataloging-in-Publication Data available upon request.

ISBN-10: 0-8027-9569-2 (hardcover)
ISBN-13: 978-0-8027-9569-4 (hardcover)

Book design by Ian Butterworth

Visit Walker & Company's Web site at www.walkeryoungreaders.com

Printed in China

2 4 6 8 10 9 7 5 3 1

All papers used by Walker & Company are natural, recyclable products made from
wood grown in well-managed forests. The manufacturing processes conform to the
environmental regulations of the country of origin.

Winston the Book Wolf

Marni McGee

Illustrations by

Ian Beck

WALKER & COMPANY NEW YORK

Winston the Wolf swished his tail as he ran past the burger stand. He *did* slow down to sniff, but he did not drool.

Meaty treats were not what
Winston had in mind.
Winston wanted books, and
he knew where to find them.

He marched up the library steps and saw a handwritten sign.
"Words!" he exclaimed. "Yum!"

NO
WOLVES
ALLOWED

He snatched the sign and **ate it.**

Winston opened the door, but an angry librarian stood in his way. "You, Mr. Wolf, may **not** come in. The sign on the door says: NO WOLVES ALLOWED."

Winston bared his teeth. "I ate your silly sign," he growled. "Now step aside."

The librarian rang her bell.
"He's back," she cried,
"that wicked wolf who chews on books!"

Library helpers came running. Winston tried to dodge them, but soon everyone was chasing poor Winston the Wolf.

Winston leaped over computers, hopped over tables and chairs.

Soon he'd be **trapped.**

But then a girl named Rosie appeared.
"Quick," she said. "Follow me."
Rosie showed Winston a secret door.

She led him through an alley, then under a bridge, and over a hill.

When at last the two of them
stopped, Rosie demanded the truth.
"Why do you nibble on books?
Why ask for trouble, Wolf?"

"Isn't it obvious? Can't you guess?"
asked Winston. "Words are **so** delicious!
Why, words taste better than roasted
skunk, even better than gopher stew!"

"Wolf," said Rosie,
"you must break this terrible
habit. You must Never nibble
on books again. Never!"

Winston began to howl.
"I'll starve," he wailed.
"I'll *die* without words!"

Rosie just laughed. "Be quiet, Wolf, and listen to me. You do *not* have to chew on a book to taste the wonderful words inside. Words taste even better when you eat them with your eyes!"

Winston squinted at Rosie.

"Is this a trick? Can this be true?"

"Trust me," said Rosie. "Sit down. You and I are going to have lessons."

So each afternoon, Rosie read **stories** to Winston.
She taught him to sound out the words.
Winston caught on fast. He learned to eat words with
his eyes, which is to say: Winston learned to **read**!

The hungry wolf ate all sorts of words—sweet and juicy words

like **sunset**

and **swoosh**

and **rambunctious.**

He wolfed down words like

trickle, icicle,

and *pickle.*
To him they tasted like clean, spring rain.

His favorite words rhymed with *crunch*—

punch and *munch* and *lunch.*

Winston read Rosie's books until he knew them all by heart. Then Winston said to Rosie, "I **must** have a new stack of library books."

Rosie sighed. "Why try it again? You know they will block the door. The sign says: NO WOLVES ALLOWED! And that means you."

"I'll never give up on
books," he declared.
"Never!"
Then Winston smiled.
"Do you suppose your
grandmother's clothes
might fit a wolf?"

Rosie scratched her head.
"Grandma's clothes?"

"Trust me,"
said Winston.
"I have a plan."

On Saturday morning at a quarter to ten, Winston and Rosie walked to town. Winston wore a frilly, rose-print dress with ruffled lace at the neck. The skirt almost hid Winston's bushy tail, and a floppy hat disguised his pointed ears.

Perched on Winston's long snout were Grandma's glasses in thin, wire frames.

Town

When Winston and Rosie arrived, no one blocked the library door. Winston stuck his snout inside and breathed in the musty-dusty smell of books.

The librarian jumped to her feet and stared. That grandma looked familiar . . .

Rosie marched right up to her. "I'd like you to meet Granny Winston," she said. "She needs a library card so she can check out books. And she'll gladly read at Story Time – the children will love her tales."

Winston nodded.
"I'll read to the children all day long, if you like."

Story
Time

And so, week after week, "Granny Winston" read stories to children. If anyone noticed the sharp, white teeth, no one complained. And if at times the hem of Granny's skirt seemed to twitch and sway, no one revealed the secret. Winston the Wolf – or Granny, so called – never lost his taste for words. Words were always his favorite treat!

A NOTE TO THE READER:
If your Story Lady wears long
skirts and floppy hats, she may
be a Wolf in Disguise — a lover
of words, a gobbler of books.
Please be very kind — for me!

Love,

Winston the Wolf x

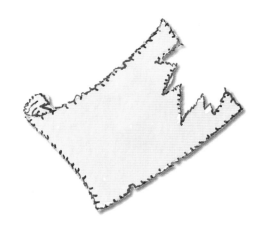

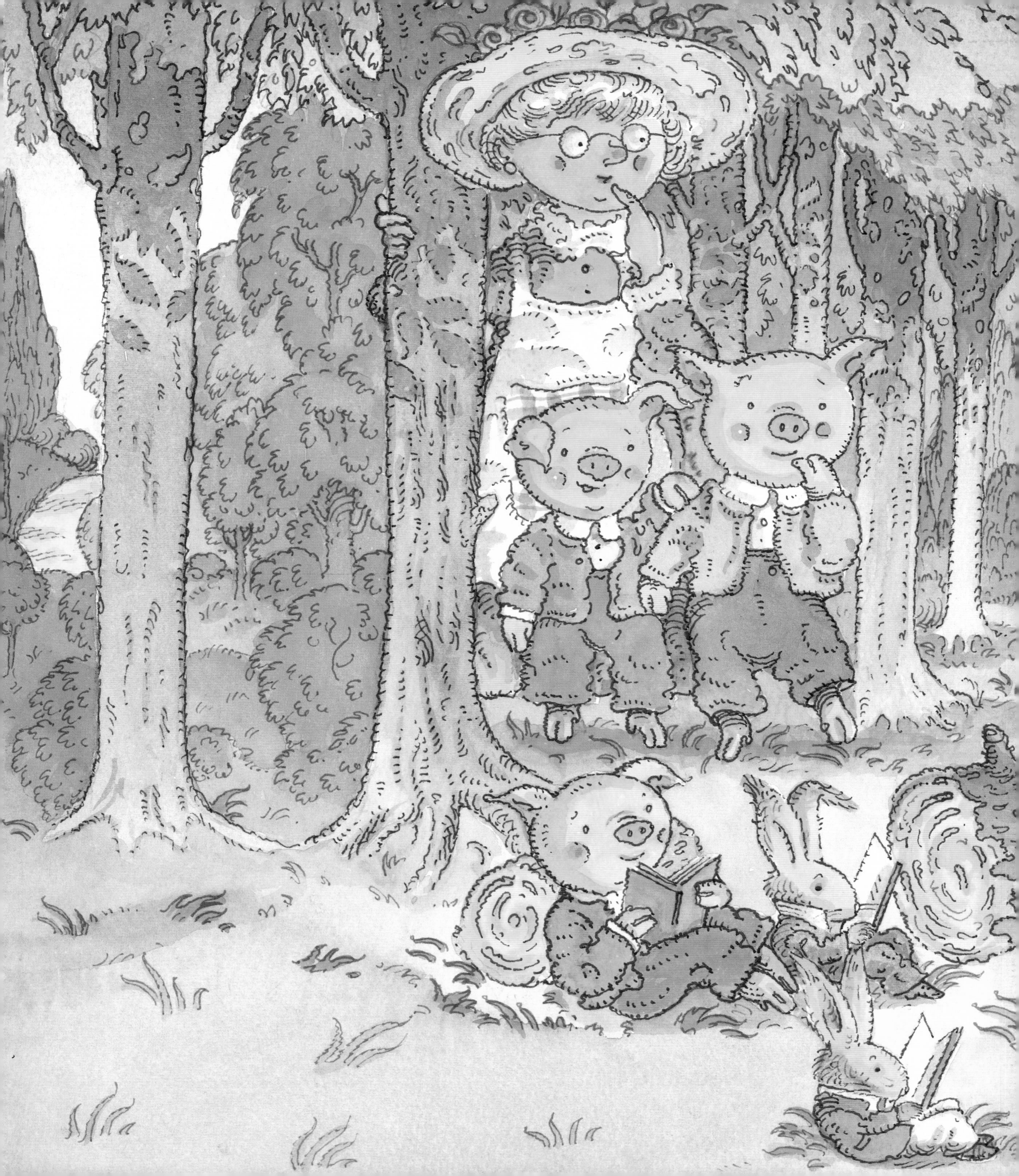